Murder

ALSO BY DANIELLE COLLOBERT, IN ENGLISH TRANSLATION:

It Then (O Books)
translated by Norma Cole

Notebooks: 1956–1978 (Litmus Press)
translated by Norma Cole

Murder

by **Danielle Collobert**
translated by **Nathanaël**

LITMUS PRESS 2013

ISBN 978–1–933959–17–7

Cover photograph: Robert Capa, *Bombed building, Spanish Civil War 1937*
© International Center of Photography. Used with permission of Magnum Photos.

Design & typesetting by Mark Addison Smith.

Litmus Press is a program of Ether Sea Projects, Inc., a 501(c)(3) non-profit
literature and arts organization.

Litmus Press publications are made possible by the New York State Council
on the Arts with the support of Governor Andrew Cuomo and the New York
State Legislature. Additional support for Litmus Press comes from the Leslie
Scalapino–O Books Fund, individual members and donors. All contributions
are fully tax-deductible.

State of the Arts

NYSCA

Litmus Press   Distributed by Small Press Distribution
925 Bergen Street #405   1341 Seventh Street
Brooklyn, New York 11238   Berkeley, California 94710
litmuspress.org   spdbooks.org

LIBRARY OF CONGRESS CATALOGING-IN-PUBLICATION DATA

Collobert, Danielle, 1940–1978 author.
  [Meurtre. English]
  Murder / by Danielle Collobert ; translated by Nathanaël.
   pages cm

  ISBN 978-1-933959-17-7

  I. Nathanaël, 1970– translator. II. Title.

  PQ2663.O5M413 2013   843'.914–DC23   2012043480

Murder

It's strange this encounter with the internal eye, behind the keyhole, that sees, and finds the external eye, caught in flagrante delicto of vision, curiosity, uncertainty. The one that looks out, to see outside itself, what is happening in the world, perhaps, or inside itself, but in a hesitant manner, so imprecise, that itself, this eye, doesn't know whether it's looking into the emptiness, into the air, into the other, or into a distant landscape, which it brought to life, like a memory, a wanted decor, chosen, an elemental power, that could be the background of its life. So this eye, sitting on this chair, watching through the keyhole, or perhaps through the slit comprised between the two slats of wood that form the back of this same chair, this eye, I say, dazzled by the sun that comes at my back, onto my back, into me, through my shoulders, heated like steel, has the power, or better, the strength to divine things. It knows how to look, on the waxed floorboards, still through the back of the chair, squatting, at the ray of sun, that falls, gliding between two slats of wood also, darkly colored, that suddenly shine with a thousand little facets, or else this eye can see, through the back of the chair, the emergence of the miniscule parasites from the wood, so old, that the patina itself appears to be innocent. The hand distends the eyelid, the eye enlarges, it is more visible, more coherent, but the vision becomes more blurred with the effort. So there is no point. We continue not to see, in the ray of sun, the tenderness, so gentle, that rises toward us, in the veins of the waxed wood, so gentle, that no arm has ever been able to grant this sensation of gentleness, to a head leaned against a shoulder, gently, tenderly, securely. We watch the rays of sun, but sitting on this chair, it might be possible to see so many other things that vertigo suddenly catches hold of me, throws me to the floor, toward the ceiling, and I climb along the oblique walls to enter into the vessels, deliberately prepared, for the new cosmonauts. It is evening, and it is impossible to discern the machines. All of this has the appearance of a drifting ship, quiet and without importance, but we are not completely confident. These foreigners who speak for us, have rapid, fulgurating departures, that we are not yet accustomed to, and the eye damages itself at this speed, and finds excuses to inform itself, and doesn't immediately allow the transformations, gigantic metamorphoses. We are so small; and what must one hold on to when one no longer recognizes one's own hands, nor one's step, nor even the small dose of everyday despair. These are painful magicians, but still very much alive. It is probable that one day, toward the end of our life, we'll think of trusting them; or at least of adopting them. These dreams of space, invented by the eye to accept the difficult abidance and reduce the distance between ourselves and the means, between ourselves and what happens, and what bears away, like a wisp of straw, at the center of revolutionary struggles, at the center of new unpredictable combats, of the unrealizable and constant suicide by little pieces, the low flame of that burn, all those distant dreams, have us spending tragic nights.

If the eye looks suddenly behind itself, if it turns around on itself, then there is the rise of each edge of the aqueous and malevolent substance that clouds it, blinds it, and terrifies it, until it can once again forget everything that happened, for it, deep down, without having that great invasive fear to overcome with each degree, with each new step, scaled like the highest of mountains, the steepest of summits.

Glitters, palpitations, splashes, pass in front of the eye, in the ray of sun, suspended, dusts. It is impossible to establish relative relationships between us, the small world, and all this contained space, without a precise dimension, in this place, in the sun. We can want to enlarge it such that even a dream would be powerless against this dimension, this form. Everything must be invented anew, down to the smallest atom, a new imaginary found as well. The chair modifies itself, can modify itself. It is no longer a chair, not even a keelson, but something useful yet, a fecund substance. The eye uses it, forges it, by oppressing me, by making use of my slow decomposition. I sometimes refuse, and we lock ourselves then in a muteness, a silence that cries: "Enough. Don't remove me from here, leave us the thick sleep, the tranquility. The new stories are not for us.

We're only able to resume our constant cycles of small sadnesses, small happy sensations—infinitely begin a love anew, then lose it, despair of it, infinitely—nothing more than the habitual stream."

But suddenly now, in the midst of repose, a newly burst flower, opens, gradually enormous, at the center of the eye, fills it, renews it. A flower, or a fence, a bullfrog, a satellite, so many other things that cannot be enumerated, we have already said so. But this is not so simple, for example when the cold of a knife blooms, some force of destruction, small though it may be, diverted though it may be from its ritual usage. Doubts surface then, more frightening than a face marked by horror, more dangerous than all poisons. The different possibilities catenate, multiply like a hydra. We lose our footing in space, sometimes empty, and limitless. We would quite like to escape these unfurlings, these plunges, but the eye, through the chair, recedes, at such a distance that its movement becomes irreversible. The step, overcome despite ourselves, also becomes the point of departure of an entire fall, in which the head rolls over itself, shudders with each inflicted shock, fractures unceasingly, reveals so much suffering that it is then necessary to try as much as possible to limit the trace left by the passage, to camouflage, to round oneself to decrease the power. And we find ourselves far from home, in a foreign country; we live there as poorly as the last of the humans who dwell there, in a desert region perhaps, or in the greatest misery. One must become accustomed to it, or else continue to live in the same manner, without knowing, or without remembering that elsewhere there still exist events, invasions. Now we look from afar, like a mountaineer sitting on a platform, his chin leaning against his hands resting flat on his staff, looking down, at the plain, the distant lights, the trace of rivers, the parceling of lands, the tentacular kernels of cities, or else it's a fisherman somewhere, in view of the coasts, barely outlined in the evening. So much distance.

How did we get here, after that strange life we led, without astonishment, even in the most unusual situations, the most unpredictable ones. We accepted it all, as a necessary thing. We were always so available, prepared to seize every pretext, every adventure. We didn't let a single chance for change pass us by. So this sudden exhaustion is perhaps also a normal thing, that was meant to come slowly, one day or another, because it is necessary to stop walking, at some point. I am not vanquished. The white marble of the table, the chair cushion, are afraid of exchanging their colors, and an old obese woman will die in the hallway behind me, in a heap of black, satined silk, several graying strands of hair falling suddenly over her eyes, in her fall, I had always known her to be so well combed, her smooth hair pulled back, in her twisted bun. My difficulty remembering stories, that happened to me, prevents me from believing in them, from finding their presence again. I was born today, you could say, but the mirrors already profess a very great age, just as men already suffer less physically after a long race. How will we find one another again, in the midst of what path.

I lean my head against the chair and I wait. I look through the slit in the back of the chair, and nothing moves anymore. Their trap. The gestures made again, that we are permitted to make again. My hand grips the back of the chair. To take it, squeeze it with both hands. But also, remove the strand of hair, along my nose, fallen. Impossibility. If I let go of the back with one hand, I fall back. I try with a movement, with my shoulders, with my head. But the head neither, I mustn't. Because of the stains on the floorboards, which I must hold in my eyes. Constraint, obligation. So everything is transformed, the chair, the street, the city, the sun. But the other one is still there, behind the keyhole, from the start. He sees me close my eyes. I am his, I am seen, exposed, my mouth agape in my sleep, and we are not very calm, because there appears, little by little, in the wall, the man who for several days now, I have decided to kill. And I would like to do it by surprise, also I hope he won't be alerted, that's why I question myself as to his presence here, at home. We will kill him in a thousand ways. I'm well versed in murder. I invent several each day. I bring different people to death, old ones for the most part, I don't exactly know why. I can't do without that game. I consider the execution of my plan, of their death, in the slightest details, but their death is not always a sufficient thing. I'm afraid of not destroying them completely. The bodies discomfit me the most, not the manner of their disappearance, of bringing them to their end, to the moment at which, definitively, it is no longer possible to speak of them. This one, I chose a long time ago. I know him well, he is, so to speak, another me, more gentle, more understanding. Together we have felt a lot of hatred that we don't forget. His hand advances and takes my neck, and gently caresses. A great goodness for me. He's barely articulating, but I understand that he wants to calm me, reassure me. He says that he knows nothing, that I can do whatever I want, that he will let himself be, without saying a thing. But I sense that he wants something. I don't hear very well. Is he afraid I'll make him suffer, or perhaps he doesn't trust me. He thinks that I won't go all the way to the end, that I'll stop in my task, continuing to pursue him eternally like this, without ever putting an end to him completely. He could betray me at this moment, in my sleep, take my throat, squeeze. But he doesn't know; and it would never occur to him, to do me harm. He remains there before me. Gradually around me, he acquires, by turning, a prodigious speed, so great that myself, at the center, I am incapable of imagining it. The millions of kilometers thus traversed, throughout my life—if they could be counted—and he in an instant—the same instant that renders my life all of a sudden so derisory, with its miniscule daily efforts—finds himself in possession of a millennial experience, a sum, all the forces of the world gathered into his hands, that choose nonetheless in this moment, the simple gesture of that caress at my neck, he so fearsome already.

I came down off the chair, and now I am crawling. The sun is disappearing, and in the suspended dust the dimensions gradually shrink, until they are level with the ground, where finally all that is left is a light, insignificant shadow. And the new promised death, in the old world, the room, the sun, this heat, which is no longer compact, homogeneous. The decomposition, gradual, inside, recent, sudden; not yet the odor that I anticipate, cold and strong, in which I will end up.

It's a very friable dough, very soft. I roll it, I stretch it between my palms, and I slide it between my fingers. I don't want to give it a definitive appearance, stop at a given stage of its transformation, also I continue tirelessly with this modeling.

People pass and look at me. I remain seated for days at a time with this earth between my hands. Sometimes, it happens that I open my palms, to let the form rest flat for several moments. It stands up, it surfaces thus, and each time, I am afraid. Also I quickly close my hands to imprison it anew, destroy it, reconstruct it. Finally entire seasons pass. Sometimes there is an accident. Twice already, I stopped, and twice in a row I recognized the same form. I was consternated. For a moment I thought my hands were developing the habit of a movement, a sort of experience. But it isn't that; otherwise I could easily stop right away; or rather not, I'm very afraid to stop now, to see that form surface once again. What to do. Right now it's winter, the dough is soft, but cold, freezing. My hands are cold too, they are becoming heavy. This leaves me a bit of hope for the third form. Thus it won't altogether be able to resemble the others.

More and more often a sharp pain pierces my right hand. And more and more often as well, I want to close my eyes, to throw the dough into the middle of the street. I know very well that if I dare do such a thing, the people all will rush at the form, thus irremediably executed. I cannot imagine their reactions. I only know three or four of them, for having seen them stare at me often behind the window panes. I asked myself several questions about them. But the answers are only deduced from their appearances. I could still affirm that two of them will take the dough and put it on a plinth, in the square of our island. The two others will want very much, on the contrary, to play a dirty trick on it, crush it underfoot. I also asked myself, whether they would do this with cruelty, in the end I don't think so. For the others, I find myself in utter doubt as to their reaction toward my clay. Maybe in fact, it is of no great importance.

I have a chance of getting out. A single chance among thousands. I remain arrested before the number of ways offering themselves to me. I don't know what to do, which path to take. This choice requires an intense reflection, and puts me in a state of very great perplexity. A single chance. Many might think that due to the infinitesimal possibility of success, I ought to make a decision whichever one. It is very much what I am tempted to do, sometimes, in moments of discouragement. But my will is strong and the choice too important so as not to have a last burst of lucidity at the decisive moment. I remain therefore in expectancy and in the fear of the irremediable. Among all the proffered paths, every day I find myself eliminating certain paths toward the exit that seem to arrive only very problematically. One must not, in any case, judge this effort of reflection to be totally futile. Of course, I may be mistaken in this selection, and an error suffices for me to lose myself. Nonetheless I have until now had faith in this logical and lucid reasoning, which guides me in these successive choices. I must add that the reduction, even minimal, of my possibilities of egress reassures me. It is quite evident that this reduction will never succeed in putting me in the alternative of a choice between one path or else another. But it remains nonetheless for me an impression of security, of protection. On the other hand, I must admit to a very guilty preference for a path that finds itself several steps from me. I don't exactly know where this preference originates. Its external aspect may respond in me to a particular taste that I would have difficulty clarifying. Regardless it must be said, this external aspect is perhaps misleading. It is possible that at the end of a very short trajectory it will change physiognomy and even direction. Yet, each morning, when I arrive before the entrances to the labyrinth, I cannot prevent myself from feeling a certain satisfaction at its sight. I stay and contemplate it thus for long hours. Still, worry soon returns, despite the efforts I make to relax, to loosen myself.

Sometimes, over the course of my long days, friends, or simply relations stop in to see me. They sit in a circle and await my words. The feelings they have toward me are quite varied. It isn't rare either for some of them to make several insinuations on the itinerary to take, or even, give me some advice, with regard to the attitude I should adopt before such and such a problem. I always listen with great attention. Very rarely, I must say, do I have the impression that these opinions can be of any succor to me, so much do they appear assured. But very quickly, I realize that they end up contradicting one another, or else they don't account, in totality, for my entire life. I am perhaps too demanding, but it's quite normal that I attach myself, in these circumstances, to the smallest of details. And it sometimes happens that these little things take on an extraordinarily acute meaning. Also I am accustomed to being suspicious, or at least, to doubting a priori all suggestions relating to my state.

The path I take every morning to reach the labyrinth is long and difficult. Sometimes I must stop for a moment along the way. These moments are painful. I'm suddenly afraid I won't be able to reach the end. I often have this impression that it is necessary for me to hurry, that each minute of absence is irreparable. A capital event might take place which might perhaps be a clue, a help to me. And yet nothing happens, even during my absence, I can confirm this, because I never remark any change, even though I don't neglect a single detail in my daily inspection. Everything is calm, empty, without rhythm. Only sometimes do I glimpse far behind me, the silhouettes of men who work in the big factory more than a kilometer from here. Their voices, which I can hear when the north wind blows, manage, for an instant, to divert all my attention. There are also, more often, the fog-horns as the boats are on their way out, in the port, at the bottom of the hill. The fog-horns. But these are all but distant noises, barely perceptible. Sometimes, on the wall of the labyrinth, I see a passing shadow. I turn around and I sense it flee. I get up, I run after it as long as I can. And when, breathless, the blood beating thunderously at my temples, I stop, the shadow then disappears between the leaves of trees, the palisades, or a garden's gates. I remember one of those pursuits, a mad chase, which came close to having quite unforeseen consequences. It was evening, the shadow was moving ahead of me, very quickly, down the hill. I raced down the slope between the dense houses, all the way to the harbor. I tripped between the crates, the casks, the iron bars strewn on the docks. The shadow stopped a moment against the wall of the last basin. Then it slid against the footbridge railing of one of the boats, whose machines had already started up to leave the harbor. I glimpsed it very high up, near the lifeboats, where it came to a halt. I hesitated an instant, then I don't know why, I made the unconsidered gesture of approaching the footbridge to climb aboard. At that moment a man in uniform emerged in the night, at the foot of the bridge. Abruptly, he asked for my passport. I raised my head, the shadow had disappeared. So I extricated myself and fled.

After such pursuits, I remain for several days in a state approaching numbness. I close my eyes, sitting in the sun, leaning against a tree across from the labyrinth. It may look like I'm napping, and yet in reality, I perceive the slightest movements of the air, the flight of an insect, and even the passages of shadows on the wall, which relax my eyelids. During these days of appeasement, I always make the resolution never to take flight again or distance myself from the labyrinth, from this path, from the exit. I don't know if one day I'll have enough strength to resist, to cease to be tempted by the shadow, to cease to want to forget the essential. A long and slow worry is gradually reborn, heavy like the drone of insects, in the heat. My body becomes strained again. I am once again on the lookout, irremediably.

Sometimes I get up with the light sensation of decision. I go toward the entrance to the labyrinth which for a long time has seemed sweet and good for me. When there remains but one step to take to leave this world definitively, to start down that unpredictable path, and perhaps finally make it out or lose myself for good, suddenly I balk, I back up. Once again, it's too soon. Nonetheless one day I will cross the threshold of the labyrinth, but toward what?

I feel as though I am experiencing a death.

I have no center anymore—not that it is repositioning itself inside me, in a continual, perpetual movement, so to speak—but it no longer has any possible location. I no longer have any integrity, unity, of organization. What will become of me thus, lost, uprooted, dislocated by the slightest abrading accident, the slightest asperity. Before it was possible for me to roll, in any situation. I pivoted on myself, I always found myself standing. Each movement, now, creates in me a very great worry. I can never predict what will remain in me, absolutely intact. It is not impossible that one day, there will be nothing left.

I flee. Every day, I take the form of a departure. There are no preparations to make. I simply decide. I rise from the place where I am, I traverse the city across its entire width. I reach the suburbs. I must go further still, along the gray walls, the murky waters, the blackened palisades. I pick up an old road that rises behind the factory. Down below, the boats slide over the black water. It's possible that I'll take one – an old rusted, grating launch. It descends the river all the way to the coal harbor, and stops against a mossy pier. I crossed the river thus, from the right bank to the left bank. Everything, on this side, is deserted. A last village in ruin is visible at the foot of a pile of coal, and nothing more. Sometimes a section of wall reveals a great sterile plain.

Groups of men walk toward the North, compact, silent, mute. There's no point approaching. I continue northward. A metamorphosis of some sort is likely to happen. I could then join one of those passing groups, follow with them the course which must be clear, precise, all the way to the end.

Progression along this plain is difficult. I move away from the river and thirst grows in me. At the beginning, an inexpressible, sticky sensation, then an invasion of viscosity. I become thirst, alone, totally. Thus do I find, in a false manner, a center, a totality. I run. I cry out on the plain. None of the men turn around of course. I seek the smallest shadow, the trace of a well, the humidity of a folded leaf—nothing. This quest, gradually, loses its meaning. I don't know if I'm giving up yet. I look in the distance at the men. How do they manage with this same thirst? I would like them to teach me. I cry out.

I must be starting to dry out. Already my voice doesn't carry. Little by little all I have before my eyes are blurry shapes. I fall. The circle closes. I'm still struggling. Everything turns to dullness. I speak of myself.

They tortured me, kneaded me, dilapidated me, trampled me. My bones are an erosion. I have no more support. I'm lying down, forever paralyzed. If someone had the idea to stand me up, on my feet, I would spread out like an enormous drop of some liquid, formless. A mass. It's a sensation that begins at the neck. My head has perhaps been spared; I can't know anymore, it's just a sort of intuition. No manifest emptiness—no pain.

When they took my wrists and when, on the anvil, they crushed them beneath the enormous stone, my disjointed hands were only traversed by a fulgurating desire for fainting, for annihilation. I'm not suffering anymore—but I am dying slowly, without end. It is not impossible that I am in the process of surviving an evil more profound than this erosion itself. Yet I can still feel my body—not distinctly, but in a diffuse, unpalpable manner. I am trying to imagine a part—my thigh, or my back, for example—but no real, powerful, sensation responds to this effort. So I don't know anything more about myself. I am waiting. I am waiting for the end. The startle.

I have a mark on my face. Also many people turn around as they pass. Who can become accustomed to such a thing. I pass by on the street. I look at people, and they, as they cross my path only have time to think of this mark, this sign, this condemnation.

It happened on the street, one day. I felt strange gazes, heavier suddenly, much heavier. There, at the street corner, in the window of an antique dealer, I saw the mark. I don't know in fact whether I looked for it, or whether this encounter with my reflection is due to chance. From that moment on, my appearance began to change. I hunched over a bit and I took the habit of dragging my feet a bit. Then my mouth transformed over the course of the following two weeks. I had, until then, an oblique fold at the corner of my lips, on the right. Now it has become a wide and deep furrow, a sort of gash. My hands too have undergone a rather spectacular change. The lines of my palms, which were very faintly marked have suddenly gained the clarity of a geographic course, and my fingers too have lengthened.

At first, I thought it was necessary to make certain arrangements. I must even admit that some of them might seem fairly ridiculous. I also enquired, as much as possible, as to the origin of this malady and the chances of recovery. In vain. The nature of this mark is presently still unknown, as for recovery, if it were to occur one day, I could only ever consider it to be nothing but the fruit of the purest chance.

I had then to come to terms with it fairly quickly. I continued to live in a sort of permanent powerlessness. My existence obviously bore no further relationship to the one that had preceded my malady. In my city, little by little, this mark established a new identity for me. I gradually withdrew to the edges of the little world in which I had lived until then, peacefully.

I have no refuge anymore, so to speak, no rest.

I took the habit of living at night. The beginning of the night always brings me a sort of strange serenity. I go into the streets, I walk at length, for hours on end, in the midst of people. I draw aside only slightly when faces approach me in full light. I avoid mirrors, too, almost instinctively. I have the impression that my body relaxes, loosens in the dark, that the mark is attenuated, diminished, that the outlines fade little by little. I would like to stop sometimes, move into the nickel lights, the violent café neons, warm myself a bit, too, sometimes. But I know that a single gesture, a single step would suffice to break the calm, the security of the night. And I must defend myself. Against everything. It is a difficult task and endless. I aggregate to the morning people. They are of no importance. They accept me. I am a bit like them, or at least I am of use to them. It is only at this hour that I can stop. I find the same itinerants, every day, a petty little Polish man, a dirty old hunchback, the old dishonored actor, with strange voices, strange hands, soft, long, little flame—without incandescence, on the verge of falling. They all play the same game, here at the end of night, their myth. They try. They speak. Stories I recognize according to their smiles, their gestures, their gazes. I listen. I know that I too could try a story out, rebuild mine, make it live again several minutes more before the full of the day, the sun, the city. But I haven't the strength, stupidly. I rise and carry on. One more time.

I can no longer speak my name. It has been a long time since I no longer can. I am not able to articulate it. I stammer desperately each time the question is asked of me, also people almost always ask me to repeat it. For me it is something unbearable. I feel as though I must extract it from the depths of myself, like spit. I flay myself, I am raw. And also often, I am naked, shameful, guilty.

Why am I disarmed thus. My name. I often find it strange that it is precisely this word that I can no longer pronounce. Is it by chance. Who knows.

I tried to transform a letter, a syllable to see. But no change, it's always the same.

Why do they all ask after my name. Sometimes I imagine another one for myself, and I repeat it at length, amorously, I could say. I even decide to adopt it, but it isn't possible. It's a question of meaning.

I don't know if I like my name. It's become a thing, an obstacle. It forces me into a constant struggle. And yet it is my good. Mine. It's probably all I have left. It's me too— on forms everywhere. Because everywhere there are forms with my name on them – in capital letters. As always.

I dreamt of writing it in a corner that was all my own. Now that's it. I am between four walls. My nails skid. The stone is hard. I dig into it with difficulty.

At first I wrote it in a corner, very small. I remembered

the walls, the palisades, the dirty walls. Between the old torn posters, the rags, the banners. Written in chalk, in charcoal, anything I could find on the ground or in my pockets. It was necessary to be careful. Sometimes a kid emerged, from I don't know where. Generally, he fled when I looked at him.

I remember all that, now, and my name written in enormous letters in the city.

Here I have started over. It's the last time. On the four walls. I have chosen the one that receives the morning sun, through the gates. In capital letters, enormous, with my nails.

Soon I will have no nails left. My hands are already bloodied. Then I will have to stop definitively.

I have an internal sea, not so big, but it fills all of me. It isn't calm water, dormant, as they say. Depending on the days, the hours, it swells, it rattles me. It follows the rhythm of the tides, mine. The waves rise and roll in my head. It rushes at my sea walls. It strikes my rocks with all its force, it surges in my caverns, the most recessed grottos, it breaks against my cliffs. Masses of foam grip the reefs. Into the hollow of the waves do my entangled organs descend.

It could drown me, break me, but on the contrary, its existence makes me live, with difficulty, it's true, because it is a weight in me, but an indispensable weight, alive.

I hear its voice, its murmur; a great internal confusion.

I think of the other one, I remember. I place myself on him, and the sea suddenly overflows, carries me from one side to the other of its body, a gentle slide like a summer sea, but a distant sea this time, with another rhythm, so gentle. I go from one edge to the other, and he thinks he is on the sea. We are stretched out on the sand where the last wave calms itself weakly and covers us with its coolness to the edge of our lips. Around us, rocking in the evening, a large bay, very calm, with islands, barely emerging, like sandbanks, covered in kelp, shrubs of thorny grasses; smells. In the low parts, marshes stagnate. From there, sometimes, headed for the open, above our heads, the flight of heavy birds, and in the sun, when it grazes the surface of the water, in the rays, golden, thousands of insects rise, above the rushes. Along the same line as his brow, small black boats pass, carrying, as they glide across the bay, their triangular sails, the color of burnt earth. Sometimes too, a tranquil and slow song reaches us from a moored boat. An infinite repose. To remain there, on the sand until the end, in the calm, the wateriness, security.

But this external sea, this great ocean gradually withdraws, far, very far from me, and I'm in the pit again.

Here is another of her inventions, she never leaves me alone. When I leave her, when I am sometimes able to do so, I go and I walk some more. She attaches herself to me, through a piece of seaweed, she wraps me up. No one can see her, but I know her, I know that she is there and that she doesn't let me go. Thus am I incapable of forgetting her existence, even at moments when it is my greatest desire. She is invincible. When I sink in somewhere, she doesn't help me, she lets me slide, she doesn't manifest herself. She would like me to forget her so that I am sucked further in, to see how far I can fall. She makes some concessions, and I drown. I'm at the bottom of the well, lost. And yet I just need gradually to get used to my hole, to take a small pleasure there, for her then to become unleashed. She pulls on the knot in which she has me caught, she lifts me with jolts. I remain suspended mid-air, with this rope cutting my body, penetrating my flesh, tearing into me. I make desperate efforts to free myself. I thrash about with all my might, but I can do nothing in this absurd position, lifted mid-body, suspended in the air at the end of the rope. I must let myself be hoisted little by little, without reticence, without refusal. I rise, I find my footing in her once more. Like a ship, she beats my flanks as before. I am reunited with her torment, her worry, her presence in me. And then I know that I need her, indissolubly.

Caught in a trap—we've been caught in a trap. We entered there through the narrow passage that leads to the cages of wild cats. And then the arena. I saw it half full as I was entering. We became imbricated the ones inside the others, like the wheels of a machine.

Our mass increases, it is discernible by the slow wave of suffocation that reaches us by the nape of the neck, coming from far behind us—transmitted by each body, to the other body, to the other middlings.

Fear. All the possibilities for destroying us. They have all the possibilities, against us. Our powerlessness—our voiceless howls—our too burning flesh, too entangled. A single breath.

The heat increases—the pain increases—insensitive beginning of madness, panic. The great fear of being killed by them. Already, at times, the question of knowing how—to appease oneself.

To kill us all—or else to refine our torture, to kill only one—to show us.

If he dies at last—at the center of us all, at our midst, or even overhead. We watch—violently—there is nothing to see. This man—who is us—in blood, ceases his twisting.

From his open body, little by little, the sanguinolence of his entrails, his spilled brain, reaches us—the horror in the hot puddle of our sweat, which is already devouring the first corpse.

We made a circle. We trampled him, covered him gradually, by walking in the half-rot, his, our own. From the stomach, it reaches the hands, the head. There remains the odor of our first corpse—triumphant.

All around, barriers, and them. But at the center, the poor, deprived beings, in fear, and already, the blood—alone— together—with the same fear, and already, the same blood.

They are capable of everything—yes. They have already killed us. Finally, they killed one of us, here. We can do nothing.

How will they continue. We can howl with fear. We cannot.

Some already, are dead, standing. They remain hooked into the compact mass, like a retrospective will not to die, to remain with us until the end—ours, together.

We barely notice them. There is their terrifying gaze— eyes rolled up, chilling.

They are caught in the slow undulation of our whole entire paste. They won't move again. Those as well, we are going to devour them, little by little. In our flesh will theirs commingle, hotter and blacker, so that we can no longer live without them, or die, without giving them back their flesh, their blood, as to ghosts who wander without peace.

We came this far to die. What a road. For all of us, what a sum of roads. Add countries, origins, different seas, the changes of the sun, the winds, the lands—and the streets, for each, the faces, the gazes.

All of this, in our masonry, the savage agglomeration of our distress. And in the eyes of those who remain—the living—a breath, a long pant, but not a word, not a sign. Yet we recognize one another. Maybe it takes place in the middle of the brow—not in the arms, nor in the hands, we know this, because our limbs are melted between them, with our bodies. So no gestures either, presences, everywhere.

What is happening now inside the head—now—to me. A memory. The terrace. Above, the other houses – the whole city, above, asleep. And the wind. An immense and fresh lightness, enveloping, sweet; the beginning of heat. In the distance, the gleam of the sea. A movement, in the distance, searching. Closer, just below, the beginning of life, waking. Several silhouettes, with cars full of fruit, that leave the train station, turn left. In a wall, an opening of electric light; in front, a table with two chairs, two seated men a bowl of sorgho in their hands. From time to time, they speak. The first odors of the day. Eyes closed. End of memory.

New pain. Fear resurfaces. Quick, quick, change immediately, think of something else. It's a struggle, a sprint. Resist allowing the fear to widen, to spread through me, run everywhere, icy cold. Raise a wall, fast, very fast—a matter of speed—but it defends itself. Take it by the throat, the way we are taken, and squeeze, squeeze. But it triumphs. So, once more, howl.

New cycle of fear. The beginning, near the house. I walked all the way to the wall. I returned toward the street. The impasse is brief, some thirty meters between the back wall and the street. A hundred times this walk from the wall to the street, with the moist cold at my back. Finally, late at night, they came to take me. I was waiting for them. Why not have left. And them, the others. They were waiting also. No, not all. Many defended themselves. There are on their faces the remains of expanses tumefied by blows, the swellings, the cracks, the bloody scabs on the wounds, the gaping openings of injuries. Those may no longer be afraid. They already know—on the quiet. These are the most silent among us, the most calm. Their gazes don't see anymore. They are so distant. In other sufferings, other tortures. They don't hear anymore, either, the blasts that are gradually bringing down the exterior circles, and which are coming toward us, inexorably, at the center.

I haven't spoken enough about this odor. Still, for some time now, it is all that exists really. Everything melts into it.

It isn't properly speaking a real odor, like one can smell everywhere, in the streets, in rooms, in all the houses—it's a memory-odor, a reminder-odor.

It attacks the head, envelops, clutches. I bathe in it confusedly. I found it, it grabbed me in a train. It was full of people.

I was near the door. I could thus see the landscape pass by, but only between two heads, from behind, very close, at the edge of my face. Their necks, the texture of the distended skin, the layered hair in flakes of shadow. Bite slowly, sideways—hard resistance—fill the mouth with that hot swelling sensation.

My hands started to rise along their backs, to their necks, and I squeezed one in each hand, very hard, until they were completely immobilized. I didn't see their faces, but I thought that they must gradually have become crimson, violet, incandescent. They remained without a word, without a cry. No one noticed anything. They remained stiff against the door.

The odor arrived at that moment, from them, and then also from a small slit, in the wood, above the door, a whistle of air. Both the noise and the odor. It was the noise at first that I wanted to flee, not the odor. The odor, immediately, imposed itself, thus, naturally.

I looked around me; it was difficult to move about, I realized this immediately. I folded my arms against myself, drawing my shoulders in a bit, and I tried to pour myself between the people. It was a long road, troubling touch, sometimes approaching embraces. Air holes opened in places, formed by the masses of suitcases, and I had to stride or scale.

I walked in contraflow, a perpetually broken equilibrium. Several times, the passage past the buffers, between two cars, arrived like a plunge into the night. I had to rush, in that movement, the clicking steel, without seeing, without looking, with the fear, suddenly, of pitching.

I arrived at the end of the train, later. Something had to be done. I could not remain there, before this mobile, definitive wall. I searched for a bit, then I opened the door and I went out, full of the odor, for a long time.

I entered into the café and I saw her immediately at the back, facing me. I stopped right away. I felt as though everything had fallen silent, that everyone was looking at me, that they had understood everything. I felt shame, as though I had entered naked into the café. I also thought I heard a snigger. Yet now I know that none of this happened. No one paid any attention to me, when I stopped near the door, to my immobility, my shame.

She was sitting, with her eyes in smoke. An old woman, a very old woman, and the resemblance. Is someone able to notice this extraordinary resemblance between this old woman and me. I am perhaps the only one to have seen it. She herself didn't notice anything. She continued to gaze vacantly into space, then she got out a piece of paper, marked it with several lines. She shoved the paper into her pocket. There were no free tables. I leaned against the bar. I couldn't help but watch her. Her. If I could have known, everything, from the start, from that moment on, entirely mine, all the way to her, at her life's end. What a road. I don't dare speak of the relation with the one I have yet to travel. What next road for me. There could be a sign, a reflection.

Her face was withered, furrowed. Her wrinkles were where I sometimes imagine them to be on my next face. From the wings of the nose to the tips of the cheekbones.

Tiny little fanned wrinkles, in the blue skin. Two big deep half-circles around the mouth. The bottom of the face weighed down, creased.

No questions about her, but a very close bond that was beginning to integrate me into her existence.

She rose. She took a briefcase of torn leather under her arm. She shoved her hands into the pockets of her old green trench-coat. I followed her for several steps. It was still fairly early in the night, and the boulevard was full of people. She was walking quickly. The tails of her trench-coat floated on each side. I watched her feet, for a long time. Her shoes were heavy, thick soled.

It was necessary to keep up, but sometimes a group of men slowed the pursuit. I could see her flow among the people, and from the start I was afraid of losing her. At first I had the impression she was dragging me toward a specific place. Then I felt her hesitate. Over what. The place, the necessity, or else perhaps she didn't know where to go.

I hesitated as well. At least, I made the motions of hesitation. I experienced the hesitation without purpose, with feverishness.

She stopped at a street corner and approached a bus stop. She must have been in the habit of taking it. She didn't raise her head to know the direction. Does she think she'll take the bus. I go to the left. There's a bench. I'm at the edge of the bench. I see her sideways, in profile. A strand of hair falls from her chignon onto the nape of her neck. Her hair is colorless. Perhaps a bit red. She must be cold. I can feel it. Yet it isn't visible. She looks at the ground.

A small round man is next to her. He's looking at her. He's looking at her feet also. A young woman is reading a newspaper behind her. To the left of the bench there is a fire hydrant. In the window I see all four of us. The image is too small for me to make her face out clearly. I would like to approach but the bus arrives. She doesn't move. The bus moves past her, stops in front of me. She comes off the sidewalk. She climbs onto the platform by leaning on her right arm. She goes to sit inside. I have to go too, but this time she may notice me. Across from her, there is a free spot. I would like very much to sit near her. I am on a wheel, uncomfortably seated, too high. She pulls a crumpled, limp booklet from her pocket. I can see her detach two tickets. A stroke of luck. Her face is strangely modified in the reflection from the lights. We cross the Seine. She looks at the water.

I calm down.

We enter a quiet neighborhood. Few people on the streets. I wait. The bus rides along in shadow.

She is going to get off. She is standing in the aisle. I wait. We are nearing the stop. I get up. I am behind her.

She follows the sidewalk. The street descends. I cross. I slow. The street is calm. I don't know this neighborhood. She is walking more heavily, a bit bent. What if she went home now. I am afraid. I would not want for this to end right away. We must be approaching the docks. My heels are making too much noise. I try to slide my feet as I walk; from the tip of the foot to the heel. I'm getting tired. From time to time it resonates in the street. She must hear. I don't know if she is thinking of the noise, of someone walking behind her.

I'm hungry. I notice two or three lit restaurant dining rooms. At a street corner a hundred meters away, there is a tobacconist. I feel her dig through her pocket. Her left shoulder stoops a bit. Is she going to stop. I imagine she is going to stop.

She pushes the door. I stop. I have to wait a bit. If she doesn't sit down, she'll come back out. It's possible too that she will exit through the other door, onto the other street. I walk to the corner. I can see her inside, near the counter. She is standing, with her back facing. I'm in full light now. I'm too embarrassed. I don't know what to do with my arms. My pockets are too high for me to put my hands into them with ease. I will go in.

She sits down. I enter. She doesn't see me.

The benches are gutted in parts. It's dirty. I notice right away. The papers on the ground. The little old people, very old, very old, gray, yellow. The odor as well. I notice that I am well dressed, too well. I shall have to do something. I hunch over my table. I become heavy, thick. My face as well.

I haven't yet seen what she ordered. For once I order some

white wine. I never order wine in cafés. Here, it's natural. The server doesn't seem surprised. My hands have turned gray. It's a bit because of the light, white, decomposed.

A piece of scratched mirror, in a corner. A bit of my face. I become ugly. Usually, I watch myself, but here everything is laden, the teeth, the nose, the eyelids especially.

She is across from me. This time we look at one another. She sees me. I regret it. I'd prefer for her not to know. Anyway, she doesn't seem to know yet. Not even a doubt. She slips elsewhere.

I drink. I should have ordered a coffee. I have the impression she'll play a very tight game. I don't know if I can take it. A coffee always makes me very vigilant. This evening, it will no doubt be very necessary. I keep an eye on her. I ask myself where the fault is. She drinks, like me, the same thing. She is sitting at the back of the bench, her legs a bit apart. She is skinny, very skinny.

I feel the filth rise along my legs. It's a feeling I caught like an old illness, on a Spanish train.

We are cold. All of us. The old people as well.

How long will we remain here. An absurd question. I know right away. There's no more time. Emptiness. Presences. She looks at me. This time she is thinking of me. She must be telling herself something about me. We isolate ourselves. For very little time in fact. She leaves again.

She feels the strand of hair on her neck. She raises an arm, her hand feels the back of her head. She pulls on the strand that falls back. On her arm which has exposed itself a bit, I see a blue number.

Now, I know something about her. I look at her. I apply a sort of formula. In fact, I settle suffering into her face. It's already there, but not in the same place. I am mistaken. I invent. Never have I suffered in my body. I can't know. I want in a cowardly way to imagine. To participate. She shakes her head no. She's right. Now it's over. Everything becomes signification. It is no longer possible.

We stay there a long time. Hours probably. She got up and I followed her. Now I am following her like a dog, simply. She must know I'm following her. She doesn't pay attention. A night bus. A stop very far away, outside Paris. Shadow. We walk in shadow. I am behind her, very close. Suburban streets, deserted, sinister also. We're walking slowly. Detached houses, old buildings. She turns at street corners which must resemble one another.

She pushes on a door. There is a very faint light, somewhere. She goes up. I am downstairs. I wait. It is understood. Then I go up too. I'm out of breath, I think. The door is open. She's on the bed, in a trench-coat, her gaze is fixed. I look at her for a time. I must go. She's dead. I look at her. I go back down. The door doesn't close. I am lost in the streets. The drizzle turns milky blue. The day is torn.

The birds swoop down onto the ground. The enormous crab empties little by little. A small gray trickle runs between the two big claws, and digs a miniscule furrow in the humid and sallow sand. The first gull advances heavily. Its beak taps against the red shell, once, then twice. A beat. The two other birds remain immobile. The gull leans its long neck back, its head raised toward the sea, then its beak lowers again slowly and slides to the side to lift the barely open wall, out of which another bubble of drool escapes. A long cleft has torn the cuirass of the disemboweled crab. Five or six beaks have introduced themselves into this fissure, and are widening it, spreading it, ripping it.

The wind has lifted the light feathers. The backs of the waves become iridescent before breaking several steps from the birds. The sand dries in places and becomes dull. Several birds swoop down along the edge of the waves, others approach the corpse. Suddenly, it starts to rain. Large drops are crushed into stars. The beach is the color of lead. The yellow belly of the crab is caved in, ripped to bits. The white and gray flesh is crumbling. Gulls fly low, skimming the water, screeching. Behind the rocks, at the end of the beach, a black silhouette walks on the flat stones covered in seaweed, wrack. It reaches the sand, advances slowly. It's an old woman who walks with difficulty, with a big bag on her side. From time to time, she lowers herself, scratches at the sand with a piece of iron and draws from it almost each time a shell which fills her hand and which she clasps hard before plunging it into the bag; or else she goes all the way to the water, and removes with a slip of the fingers, the thick layer of sand stuck to it. She has tightened the swath of her shawl a bit in the tie of her apron. The bottom of her skirt is also stained with sand. Little by little she approaches the crab. Several isolated birds have already flown off. Then suddenly all the others fly away toward the sea, in a movement cast toward the earth. The crab continues to empty itself onto the trampled sand. The old woman looks at the crab, leans forward, grabs it by a leg which hangs to the side, dismembered. The leg breaks. The crab falls back heavily. She takes it by one of its big claws, turns it onto its back. The little old woman tears off the legs and scrapes the inside with her spoon. A gray mud, almost liquid, falls onto the sand, runs toward the sea. She goes toward the water, plunges the crab, shakes it, scrubs it. She has placed her bag on the ground and pulls a piece of fabric from it. She rubs the back of the shell, then drops the rag into the bottom of the bag, and slides the crab onto the shells. She picks up her bag and starts off again taking small steps toward the far end of the beach, toward the path that leads to the village. The beach remains deserted. The birds fly in the distance over the sea. At a certain place, in the middle of the beach of smooth and uniform sand, dark marks are visible, a small mound of crab legs, gray mud.

Between two rocks, a bit of sand, a bit of mud. He is wearing pants and a big blue canvas jacket, bleached by the sea water, rubber boots and a big black béret on his head. He is bent, folded in half and is digging through the sand with his hands. The sand blackens as soon as it is exposed to the light. The hole deepens. His hands reach the layer of moist, viscous mud. One feels that he is drowning in this work. Little by little he absorbs the humidity. He concentrates. He penetrates the mass of silt, sinks in all the way to his shoulders.

But gradually, he relaxes, he finds the body, open, in the silt. A mixture of flesh and silt. He dives with avidity, but also as though with a certain rite, a familiar ceremonial. With his whole hand he takes the heart, rips it out and gets back up. He goes toward the sea, bathes it there, cleans it gently with his old tanned hands. He squeezes it lightly, a gray liquid emerges, reddish. He looks at it, turns it over, rolls it in his hands. He choose a flat stone in the sun, places the heart on it, gently, and returns toward the body. He covers it with silt, with mud, with sand, packs this earth, with his boots, erases the trace of his steps, sits on a rock and looks at the sea.

The boat approaches, coming from very far, right across from him, straight at him. He is surprised; it is visible on his face by the raised eyebrows. It arrives slowly, inexorably.

He slides to the ground, flattens himself on the sand, crawls all the way to the rock where he raised the heart, in full sun, as on an altar, takes it, looks around, seeking a refuge, and in the end stuffs it under his jacket, against his skin, with a very faint shiver. He goes toward the rock which juts the furthest into the sea, rises to the tip, spreads his legs a bit and crosses his arms over his chest, without pressure. He waits, he is ready. The boat moves forward in the sun, then he realizes it's empty, it arrives pushed by the wind, toward him. He is reassured. He smiles. It will approach the edge, touch the sand listlessly in an almost smothered screech, and come to a halt in the last little wave. He can take it, and leave with it. He'll be able to relax at last, after all these days of tension, of quest, of deep digging with his hands, with all his strength concentrated, knotted.

With this will to find, to go to the end, to not spare himself, he must have torn himself apart, intensely. Perhaps more than ever will he not have the strength to start over. It is too big a risk. His life is surely in question. It isn't something to be taken lightly. And when the game is over, the end of the torment, when the calm returns, there is no assurance that one has not, in reality, lost everything.

They left the ropes, all along the harbor. They pass from one house to another, coil half way up the walls. In the rings anchored there to keep the beasts from the country.

It's hot. Summer is approaching, and yet they haven't removed them. The hands continue to slide over them, but in this season the pressure is gentle, light, barely a caress. In winter, when the sea unleashes itself, when the wind blows and howls, when the shingles and the gulls of the beach invade the street running along the harbor, from the house at the edge of the main street to the concrete building at the foot of the lighthouse, no one walks upright. From one house to another, the men brace themselves, against the walls, clutching the rope with both hands. Sometimes their boots slip on the seaweed, or else the shingles collide between their feet. There are dangerous passages, a gap in a street, on its way to the harbor, the entrance to the factory with the crates, the lobster pots, the nets. Much care must be taken. It's a difficult road during the storm. Only the strongest risk it, as well as the elderly, who would never agree to take another path. The ropes, under the tanned hands, tense, twist between the rings, then fall back limply at the end of their effort. These ropes are necessary. How many were swept away as soon as they let go, or even scarcely manifested a certain disdain for this offered help. On the face of it, this contempt can seem quite ridiculous, and yet what force is in this desire to walk alone, upright, from one end of the harbor to the other, directly into the storm. Trying to be upright, alone, against the sea, alive, powerful, mortal.

We are four around him. He's dead. In the open field, strangely, in the open, under the sun, gently.

Nothing tragic happened. The sounds of the countryside did not stop, suddenly. He fell to his knees, then he collapsed onto his side. Such that we could envisage him, his face toward the sky. We were caught unawares, standing. One of us leaned forward, called him—lost voice—he gently slid his arm under his head to lift his body, but he let him fall back, powerless. He looked at us. He stood up. We were immobile—a long time. Him empty, emptied, incredibly empty. His body, there.

We place ourselves on the grass, around him. We look elsewhere, or else we look at him sometimes.

They get up. They lift him. The first one takes him on his shoulder. We walk behind him. His arms hang, we can see the top of his head, his brow.

The prairie slopes. We climb heavily, without completely extending our knees. The first, loses his balance, from time to time, from one foot onto the other, then he finds his balance again. Sometimes someone else holds him up. We arrive at the top of the hill.

And then suddenly, at the top, there is no country before us, but an immense city, a city in a hollow, offered, rutilant, with buildings, enormous steeples resplendent in the sun.

From where we are, a street runs toward the low houses,

it seems to go all the way to the heart of the city, swelling, widening, encasing itself in the buildings, toward the center. We have not decided to go down toward the city, but where do we go with him.

The first house is an old café. We sit outside, on yellowed iron chairs. We sit him down as well. His head falls back, stiff.

A woman passes by, stops, looks at us, leaves. She is taking tiny little steps, with difficulty.

Soon others stop. They will end up doing something bad. So the first one rises, takes him onto his shoulder. We follow him. He is the one who decided to go down toward the city; surely, we didn't all care to. But there are things to attend to.

The street descends very quickly, and its old cobbles cause us to stumble. We have to take turns. We are less strong than he is and we must carry him two at a time. He caves in. So as not to see him, the others walk in front.

We have been between the walls for a long time. We start to sing quietly. We are approaching. The disquieting approach, toward the heart of the city. Approach slowly, with suspicion; but still go there directly, because it is necessary and there is no recourse. Strange procession.

We are at the center of the city. A privileged house, high, imposing. We haven't crossed the threshold. We were in the middle of the street. A woman came out. She looked at him, she said to us "it's him, oh yes, it's him". She took him from our hands as though he were for her, weightless, and she took him into the house. The door closed, against silence.

We were in the middle of the street. There were protestations, noise. We continued our walking, one behind the other, on each sidewalk. For kilometers, the road climbs back up through the city. We don't see anything. Perhaps as well, we don't think anymore. We were with him, the dead man. We carried him, but no common word was spoken by one of us, for all of us, for the others, in the name of the others. How this death mattered for each of us, not knowing, not surmising; we just search. Death in the midst of us. Were we all in danger.

We removed him from our circle, led him through the city. A big adventure, like a very distant voyage, with perils, obstacles, walks especially, long and grueling. Walks especially, because it is important. In the obstacles, one forgets; but the feet that walk, the heaviness, it's better, it's more alive. We may not remember much more, but exhaustion always leaves something of a mark. We now have the memory of a beautiful exhaustion.

We arrive at the city limits, on the hill across from the hill of our departure. We recognize the way taken together. The task is over. Another beginning would be necessary, a new spring, or a repetition.

Returning, with the brutal passage of time, in the rupture of space, toward this city, suddenly arisen, without reality—our trajectory through it—and its imminent disappearance, without reason, because we are going to leave.

What happened in the city is still there, at our feet, without our having given a purpose to that death. Here, now, there is silence, above the city. But over there we can hear a siren wailing.

The square was completely deserted, because of the heat. An intolerable light. Only, on the left, a thin strip of shadow cut according to the height of the houses. When one arrives, along the dark vaulted corridor that leads there, one must stop dead. Flat-out furnace feeling; but at the same time, a certain lightness, a thought of evaporation.

A small bell chimes, like inside a church. In the opening of each door, people are standing, immobile, wearing black, old women, especially. The square is closed like a circus, or an arena—a comparison which in fact has nothing to do with this aspect of the closed place, because its own form tends toward an almost perfect square. Sometimes people entered into the square, realized there was no way out, and followed the same path out under the heavy gazes of the people of the square.

Some didn't dare penetrate into it; timid, oppressed people. Those who entered there were similar to flies in a spider's web. The passage did not take place brutally. They went from the shadow of the alley to the dazzle of the square. They closed their eyes and continued to walk. When their eyes became gradually accustomed to the light, when their eyelids opened with a jolt, then, it was already too late. They found themselves in the middle of the square, near the well, with all the gazes fixed upon them, as though ready to lose their immobility. There was then an infinite diversity of reactions. To consign them, it is probable that among the people of the square, somewhere, there must be an observer. One of the most obvious manifestations was generally the stumble that surfaced suddenly in the gait, hitherto slow and regular, and then a whole arch, an almost immediate stiffening of the whole body, very visible, too visible. Panic. Then, either the will to conceal it, believe that it was possible to play the game, or total powerlessness, which ended in immobility, the gaze overcome, stalked.

On that day, that's what it was. But in addition, this man was expected. He arrived, perhaps with some caution, himself, because regardless, he always walks with some caution; not hesitation, but on the contrary a sort of permanent tension in his walk. Before entering into the square, they felt his gaze, even before he entered into the light. He still had the possibility of not crossing the threshold of that zone—perhaps not for that matter, even though he arrived there by chance.

He had no possibility of defending himself. He entered, stunned. It was the easiest way to put him in that state of necessary inferiority. To close the eyes. For several seconds, to be their prey, and to think one is their prey. What do they do in that instant. They put chains there, cover the square with sharpened stakes, light incandescent cinders here and there, release all sorts of minuscule reptiles, insects, mollusks. One only becomes aware, of all that, by opening the eyes again. It happens in the greatest silence, the appearance of immobility. The air remains without vibration, all around.

He, is suspicious. He does everything he can not to close his eyes; his face deforms itself, in vain. He already recognizes the hostility.

In the night, he advances as far as the well. Then does the drone begin for him, almost imperceptibly, the very gentle rocking of the people of the square, a movement of shoulders, just. He parted his eyelids, then he opened them, little by little. His fear, at the center. He stops. Find fast—a fulgurating space, the time of a scream—the possibility of flight. The exit. Nothing.

The fear transforms itself, becomes a fear of them, really. He will not take another step. The ground begins its burning vibration. He foresees, he already knows, to the end. But he is still surprised by the suffering. He doesn't call for help. He bends, folds over his knees; his hat falls to the ground, bounces, ridiculous. A straw summer hat, almost white. His knees touch the ground at last, on the reddened stone. First scream, dry, almost unexpected. He wants to get up, leans on his hands, on the ground, but they are immediately absorbed, dissolved. Up to his knees his clothes burn sticking to his skin, in a single same fire. And so at length he howls. But his scream resembles a moan, he remains without echo between these walls. Half consumed, for him other tortures near. They have left the doorways and they are slowly advancing toward the center.

Only then does he notice the drone, which gradually rises in him, invades him, when they form around him a thick, consistent, circle, but so to speak, invisible, then, one last time, does he look at them, and release at last, the first sob.

He is a small man. He is dark, his complexion a bit yellow, his skin flabby at the base of the neck, as with many middle-aged men. He lives near one of the city gates, in a grayish hotel. He has always lived there, at the hotel, in this hotel. Perhaps not. The elevated rail runs at the height of his windows, the bedroom window and the one in the little recess where the sink and the electric heater are. The recess is separated from the room by a floral curtain, half yellow, half pink, it isn't clear exactly. The room is impersonal, no objects, little things. A gray wardrobe, suitcases covered with a piece of green fabric. There is paper with big flowers, a bit like the recess curtain. Early in the morning the train goes by and he watches. He makes small precise gestures, familiar, always the same. No singular, unusual movement. He shaves, combs his hair. The water is heating. Smell of coffee. On the table near the window, his cup. He drinks. Other smells in the establishment, the smells of coffee throughout the hotel, through the open windows, in summer. Right now, with his cup, he's watching the train, he's thinking about it. People go by, standing, very tall, hanging from the bars, emergent from sleep. Faces, endlessly. The whole time the train goes by, he watches. He can't see the faces. He thinks of this.

He puts on a gray raincoat, a hat. He is old. He goes down the hotel steps. He walks on the central divider strip, beneath the train. He walks for some time all the way to the gate, the suburban bus stops. He doesn't recognize anyone. And yet there are markers; people chanced upon every morning at the same hour, for years as well. The same people. Children who grow up on the way to the nearby lycée. Different men and women, in the morning. New absences. He sees nothing. The bus leaves, and immediately the procession of blackened brick walls begins, the factory smoke-stacks, the warehouses, the workshops. Further along, something else. Narrow streets, straight and clean, the gardens of detached houses. Calm, in the sun. He gets off. A small workshop. Half-light, precision work, without speaking, discreet.

Return, in the evening, the winter night. The same way. The facades of the poorly lit detached houses, the edges of the city, the first neon lights, then the furious neons, the throng, the big foreign crowd, thick, sweating. It flows.

Hours of emptiness also. Cinemas. The square. Time, sitting with the newspaper, the radio, and then, sometimes as well old photographs scattered in a black box.

Home without waiting. No women either, not even brief affairs.

Flat, viscous memories. Sometimes, in passing, noises in the hotel. He is calm.

He tires. He tires quickly, more and more quickly. Almost a pain. It rises in his arms, through his nails. It stops at the nape of his neck. It stills itself. He remains seated then for hours, or even, sometimes, he lies down, his arms stretched out at his sides, frozen, unsleeping. The exhaustion passes. He starts up again.

One day he receives a call. It is a call for a young dead man, in the provinces. He goes, he leaves everything, or else he continues, following, it seems, a general line.

He watches the trees pass by, very quickly. It's a fast train. Then the bus, on the small roads. The city in which he stops in the morning is still asleep. A small provincial city, gentle, warmed by the rising sun. Silent houses, with closed gardens resembling the gardens of cloisters. Several outlines.

The house of the dead man is near the presbytery, almost the same gray house. Some people from the family, distant members. The young man is in uniform. It's striking. A young dead soldier, who is here, now, has returned.

Later, exchanged words, almost nothing. He doesn't know what to say in such cases. He remains standing without saying anything. Then the march behind the coffin, the midday meal at which he isn't listening anymore. The farewells at the train station, the return, the other train station. The subway, the hotel. Nothing new. He's tired. Very tired. He is sitting down, he takes his head between his arms in a strange way, entangled. He squeezes hard, as though suddenly it had become a block of stone placed before him.

The train passes in front of the windows, fast, very fast.

He thinks of the dead soldier. A subway. A train full of soldiers. Fast. Soldiers' faces.

The vice tightens, slowly. The yellowed paper on the walls turns to gray. The walls turn also.

The old man expires.

Seeing that man, playing with the door, in that way, was dizzying. He pushed the swinging door very hard, as hard as he could, it seemed. The swinging door went off to the side, in the shadow, and returned with all of its weight, with all of its speed, toward him. One might think he was going to receive it head on, that it was going to flatten against him, with all its violence. But what was strange, was that he had calculated exactly where the door would stop when he pushed it with all of his strength. It was precise, discreet too. Perhaps he had left a sort of margin, a sort of security.

A man had just passed, at a casual pace, swinging a newspaper at the tips of his fingers. He hadn't seen him. Others too passed, who didn't see him. People left him alone, he wasn't bothering anyone in fact, with his door. So, like that, he continued.

But something always has to happen, someone, passing by, rigged the game, he gave a small push to the door, a push that combined with the man's push. It came back at him brutally. The other one quickly withdrew and he watched the man receive the door, upright. He let out a small cry, too sharp. He toppled and he fell heavily onto his back, his spine broken.

Since, he has been lying there, immobile, without being able to make a gesture, not very far from the door, for his house is several steps from there; but his eyes don't leave it all day long. One can feel him vibrate from inside, when someone gets too close. People know it, so some avoid doing so.

Sometimes he can't stand it anymore; his gaze becomes cloudy, and he can't help but call out with his eyes to the first person who passes by his lounge chair.

The one he calls hesitates, approaches. With a movement of the eyelids, he indicates the door, and a motion of coming and going. It is understood. Then he watches the slow approach, the interrogatory stop toward him. He confirms by closing his eyes. The other then, pushes the door. It gives way, and comes back. But the one who is pushing it thus doesn't really realize what he's doing, it is of no interest to him. And then he always calculates too well, and the door falls weakly back.

Nobody, ever, puts the same force into it as he did, the same precision, the same love. And even this small joy of seeing the door come and go with the necessary rhythm, even that, at present, is denied him.

I saw the old man on the balcony. He wasn't quite there yet, as it happens, when I stopped. With one hand he was gripping the edge of the window, spreading it on the right in a blurred, trembling manner, with the other one he extended his cane to lean it against the window-ledge which formed a very thin step in relation to the balcony. The cane kept slipping and the window kept slamming shut.

After a time, he finally appeared completely on the balcony. All in all, he was a rather banal old man. He was wearing a hat, as though he had just been about to leave the apartment, when he decided to come onto the balcony. In the window behind him, the reflection of an armchair and a bookshelf moved each time the window banged.

He should never have gone out in this weather, onto the balcony.

His hand, that I could make out very well, was knotted but fine, very fine, quite pale and bluish. It was sliding along the balcony railing with great slowness. He turned toward the end of the balcony which was situated at the exact corner of the two streets. The four pigeons were right there, one perched on the railing, moving about on the same side as the old man, the three others, on the edge of the balcony, lower down, immobile.

The old man moved forward without making a sound; at least it seemed that way to me. He was not leaning on his cane, but only on the railing.

The pigeon walking along the balcony railing joined the others at their level. The old man continued to move forward. The pigeons were no longer moving. The old man reached their level. He let go of the railing and remained immobile. Suddenly a long raucous cry emerged from his mouth like vomit. At the same time, he gave a great blow of the cane, to the edge of the balcony, using both hands, all his strength.

At that very moment, or at the same time, or else immediately afterwards, I can't be sure, the four pigeons flew off and swooped down toward the street.

The old main remained there, leaning over backwards, for a moment, then he ran his hand through his white beard shaking his head. He set off again painstakingly along the balcony. He turned his head once more toward the street before coming down groping with his cane to reach the window-ledge.

An old man lives on the other bank. I think it will be necessary one day for me to speak of him. His house is big and I can see him from my door. I see him sometimes, sitting in front of his own door on a stone bench, immobile.

I could begin by telling his whole life story, as often, he himself does, in pieces, without coherence.

We all know he's not from here, that he spent his youth going from one city to another, all over the place. He stopped here, a long time ago, even before my birth. Our city is withdrawn from the world, and I wonder what could have made him want this exile. He has three sons. I know one of them. He sometimes spends the summer here in a boat. He's big and strong. Often I see him carry his father in his arms all the way to the boat. One day, close up, I saw his hands.

I remember his hands. They are big, and when they close, resting, his fingers join, their lines hug one another closely. I've never recognized such unity in a hand. It's a carrier hand, a receptacle, an offering. It knows how to hold; to contain as well. I quite like his hand.

Toward the end of the summer, the son leaves again. I don't know where. The old man until the beginning of winter stays in front of his house.

I passed by one day in a boat, in front of him. I stopped for a long while in his gaze. I got out and I sat next to him on the bench. For hours we remained in silence, the sun, the water.

He says "good, come back tomorrow." One ought to be able to say each word, one after the other, since that day, each especially, each gaze.

He bends his head "tell me." I don't say a thing. I smile. He taught me to smile.

He loves me. I don't know what we talked about, what we are still talking about. Have we said everything.

We've said what matters for both of us. What remains when nothing is necessary anymore—punctuation—sequencing.

He bends his head "bring me the water." He repeats "bring me the water." I don't know what I bring back to him in my hands. Impossible objects, colors, forms that don't hold in the hands, smells that pass, the gazes of people from elsewhere.

We remind one another of the world.

"It's six o'clock. We're tired. All of us. Me especially. In fact, they know it well. At around six o'clock, it's the slump, not sleep, but heaviness, in the back, the legs. I must say that I am old; well, compared to the others. Here it's mostly young people. They prefer it. The young go faster; they want to arrive. It's over for me. I do the work, just like that, quietly, but well, very well, with dignity. It isn't slowness. It's regularity. I have no choice. I've reached this point. Before I followed the hours, the slack periods, the busy hours, the sudden rush. Now it isn't the same anymore. I can no longer do that. If I had done so, it would have been over for a long time. It isn't a necessity, of course. That's the way it is, that's all.

"I continue. Only, I have to be careful. I take it easy as they say. I'm talking as though I were sick, but it's almost the same thing, when one is old; not sick, but old. In spite of everything, I am not at peace when I feel the afternoon go by, when six o'clock approaches. In short I know very well that it's my weak point. That's why I'm a bit apprehensive.

"Earlier I said that they knew, as well. I've been in the house for so long that they ended up paying me a bit of attention. So, they noticed. They didn't say anything of course, but I realized it. I could tell at first in the eyes of the girl. She's their daughter; a cute little young girl. I caught her watching the clock above the front door; she turned toward me, she looked at my stooped shoulders. I saw her in the mirror, then I turned around as well. She lowered her eyes, then she directed a poor, embarrassed smile at me. I quite understood, I lowered my eyes as well. I wasn't proud; a bit of a sense of guilt, the sense that all this, was my fault.

"I took up working as quietly as before, but I quite understood that in the house, it was already known. She must have heard talk about it, around her.

"There were other details, after. Not only the young girl, the others as well, all the others, little by little, learned about it.

"There's nothing more to do now. I don't even try to conceal it, to act as though nothing were happening.

"It's getting late. One mustn't think it's set off just like that, at a given hour, or else that I am haunted by that particular hour; no, only, it's irremediable; it happens, that's all, thus. I recognize its course, the first symptoms. At first, it isn't visible. Also, they cannot know exactly when it begins. They realize it at the second beat, but I know it before, well before.

"The feet. My feet, and my lower legs; with the desire to sit down, if only for a minute. One minute, and I feel as though it might pass, it might go away on its own. But it's impossible, I don't have the right; don't have the right to sit down. I stomp around all day. I follow the same little path hundreds of times. For young people, it's at night after a long day of work, that they feel their feet a bit.

"I have no choice but to continue. I drag myself along. I try to take tiny little steps, so that it hurts less, but it's no use. It's precisely by taking small steps that I start to feel my shoulders. Little by little, I have to lean forward, so it starts to be visible.

"At first I don't let myself go. I straighten up as much as I can. I walk like an automaton, but I can't take it for very long. It's hard to take. I end up giving in at the shoulders. At that moment, I'm already lost. I have only to see the gazes of the others, when I feel myself to be almost capable yet of straightening myself up, one last time. Every day, a new portion, tiny little portion of me, is used up. I know there's nothing I can do. I'm cold. One morning I will have to turn down the day's strain, all the strain of the days to come. I will have to leave."

I saw him crouched in the sun, like an arch, a separate mound, inlayed in the earth. From time to time, he lost his immobility, and became a rigid and abrupt form. His movements lacked bearing, and yet I guessed they were full of precision, of fantastic ability. It took me so much time to understand his gestures. They had two sorts of activities, one beginning from his hands, the other, from his eyes, so to speak.

The immobility was factitious. With two very long fingers, flat, lightly folded at the last phalanxes, he dug small holes in the sand, all around him. I first realized it, from the minuscule circles of shadow that surrounded him—as though all around him bullets had rained down, a dangerous limit.

He plunged both fingers in, turned them in the ground, then with a slight flick of the wrist, lifted the soil, which fell back like rain. He could make these movements without moving the rest of his body, still I ended up noticing, that with each bit of soil that fell, in him a sort of startle was produced, a breath—the sign perhaps of a great relief. It is likely possible to give this collapse another significance, but I don't know what yet.

With each startle, he must move over several centimeters, barely, which means that it's practically impossible to notice the rotation he is undertaking around himself. One might think, given the way I'm speaking of his gestures, that he must give, in time, a rather rapid rhythm to his movements. I can say now that the piercing of a single hole in the sand demands maybe an hour-long effort. I was very surprised to realize suddenly that I could only see him from behind—like the false fixity of a clock. I am expectant of his face.

There are one hundred alveoli, thus, now, all around him, along one same circle. When he will be facing me once more, I think he will form another interior circle, closer to himself; then others, closer, even closer to himself, for which he will always be the center. But by contracting thus against himself, it will be quite necessary, logically, that at a given time—when—he will straighten up little by little—to have this patience, this courage, also – then I will be able to see him standing, and know what he is like.

The quarries have been exposed for a long time to the open air, open-cut. Men have come to work here. What a job. What exhausted strength here. No one has ever sought the purpose. The pickaxes strike the wall. The work is divided, classified, balanced. The stone crumbles, the quarry, immensely, grows, pushes past its limits, beyond the horizon. It isn't known how many amid these workers have been able to climb upon the raised crests to see the whole. It's an idea that springs in none of these bodies. The arms strike without end. So many blows. We are now the wall, now the pickaxes, sometimes also the arms. How to be all three together, to know everything.

The wall in a half-circle is a white that approximates, at the setting sun, an atrocious hue, a grayish yellow.

Every day, the same procedure is observed. The men jab. The holes grow at the same rhythm. The alveoli dug by each worker meet at a point that seems indeterminate. The dust from the stone rises, evaporates and inlays itself also on the workers' bodies. The faces, little by little, become petrified. The forehead, the cheekbones, the lips. The eyes remain the last fold of the appearance of life. Little by little the face becomes the face of profound statues.

During this time, in the sky, at a vertiginous speed, heavy storm clouds pass. Enormous masses of a leaden gray flee always toward the same point, as though sucked into a terrifying emptiness. The storm becomes heavier little by little.

When in the evening the rain finally bursts abruptly, the water runs now only along stone men, gazeless, and gestureless.

We scored points. But always, we forget to write. Thus did we forgot. Not all of us. He walks with difficulty. His body leans to the left. A discontinuous rhythm. A beat to the left, a beat to the right, which becomes heavier. At that moment, one is afraid. But he is startled. A new beat to the right. He was in many wars, and he ended up losing his left arm. The rocking, that explains it. I'm in the passage of the hole—after a long presence, before another. I was used to the rhythm, the startle. It prevented me from leaving. Every day of rain, the gray docks, dirty, the whole length of the harbor, became intolerable. The filthy bistros as well. I stayed there a long time. I'm screwed here.

I first knew him with his arm. His two arms, I mean. He really has been destroyed. There is nothing to do. At least not now.

He sees the sea. He walks in front of me on the pier. At the end, there is nothing, not even a guard-rail. An unusual word. Here, no one has gone off the rails, it's common knowledge. He is still moving forward. On both sides of the pier, there are in the water, masses of enormous concrete blocks, out of which long rusted iron bars protrude, bitten by the sea. It is their irregularity which forms a strange, disquieting collection. I who know the pier well, I am still incapable of recognizing the signs they inscribe outside the water. I have found myself covering the pier four or five times in a row, to try to locate them. It didn't do any good. I forget straight away. He moves forward in the rain. He doesn't see the iron bars in the water, like swords. He sees the sea. Never has the pier been so long. For him, for me. We should prevent him, overtake him. Not just me. But at this moment, on the pier, there is only me. I think I must run. I forget the swords in the sea. The rhythm, somewhat emphasized on the left. I could run, stop in front of him, look at him. See. He would explain to me, or else he would invent something, an explanation, a compromise, subtleties.

The main thing is that he not look off into the distance, through me, past me. Prevent him perhaps, threaten him, even employ violence. Have in a certain sense, for once, a kind of courage. Hesitation. I try to stop seeing the irregular movement. I call the swords. For nothing. I take quicker and quicker steps to grant myself a bit of time, several moments of respite. Several moments perhaps to think, as though it were still the time of reflection. It's about him. Do something. I'm still far away. The rain strikes the face head on. The rain and the sea.

I thought of calling him; it would be immediate. An action right now. But he would not even turn around, because of the wind; because he doesn't hear anymore.

I am the wrecker. The sleeve of his jacket is slid flat into his pocket. Same rhythm. Like a lateral wall, the pier files past, without accident, flat. He advances suddenly, as if he were sliding very far. The distance becomes unlocatable.

Over there, it's the rain, the sea. I run at last. But the movement has come to an abrupt stop. The body toppled to the right, at the end of the pier. In the fall, the sleeve came out of the pocket, in the wind.

We lost one another in the crowd. At first we were holding hands. To avoid a tree, we let go. That's when everything began, because we could no longer find one another's hands. A column of people, in a line, separates us. I continued to talk to her over the shoulders of people. She was smiling, shaking her head. And then little by little, people passed in groups of three, four between us. Four and many more. So many people that in the end, after a time, I lost that woman. She is perhaps the one who didn't try to meet up with me. I am perhaps the one who didn't do enough to hold her near me once more. And yet I didn't want to leave her.

I'm sitting on a step in front of a house, at knee level of the people passing by. The crowd comes and goes. Sometimes all of them go in the same direction shouting the same words. Sometimes as well, they become threatening. They walk quickly. At regular intervals, a sort of panic scatters them in every direction. Different crowd.

Why am I not with the girl anymore. Where is she. In the crowd, surely she as well. I am sitting down. The step is hot. My shirt is sticking to me. I'm dirty, so dirty. I'm stammering. Last night is distant. I am a stranger, and I had her in my arms, naked. Her hair covered her face, her lips drew a great pleasure from me. I couldn't see her face. I felt her lips on me.

I recognize above the crowd, to the right, the tower of

the city hall. I know this part of the city well. All of it. The sidewalks, the cobbles, the heads of the merchants behind the windows.

I lived for a long time with the girl. In my head, I always called her that, from the start.

She gave me many things. But all of that, at this moment, is of no use to me. She taught me warmth. There are warm people and there are the others. We played at domesticating. I saw the way she did it. A look, first, long, heavy, very close, but meaningless. That's where the domestication took place. And then at the end, to finish, really like an end, the end of a dialogue, she smiled with joy, complicity. There were subtleties. For example, she stared, unsettled, then looked elsewhere, and returned at last, with a smile, from afar. How was she able to feel people thus. That's what was important, the little things, everything that lingers, in habit, everything that shows through.

Women pass by. In their backs her back is inscribed, her walk, falsified, deformed. But I imagine, my eyes half open. Hot thighs. Everything here is wet. Everything partakes of the hot weather. I'm mollified in sweat, stupefaction.

I failed. I wonder whether she says to herself as well "I failed." A caress. The time of a caress, very long. Yet we struggled together. Sometimes we struggled simply to survive. Sometimes, it was better. But in the end, we didn't build anything together. It must not be possible. A belief. I'm not a builder. I travel. This long stop here, in this city, in the arms of that woman, was also, one might say, a voyage. The last.

I have no strength. I grabbed hold of her and also I engulfed her, rejected her, trampled her. She didn't let herself be pushed around. She quite liked war. A funny sort of war, in the image of other wars.

I must still walk very far from here. I thought I had got into the habit of this city, but it's not true, now I know.

We were living in a suburb. In the corridor-streets at the foot of the factories. There were small pieces of earth, sometimes. They were narrow, long. Gardens. I don't know what name to give those bits of earth. In the spring I saw flowers grow there; nothing extraordinary as far as flowers go, tulips, for example. In the evening passing by, now I remember, now that I am sitting here, on the step, in my sweat, I heard noises. Blows against the earth; the differences between the blows. Mechanical noises also, because they made use of everything, those who worked in those gardens. In the evening I passed by and I could hear, but I didn't pay any attention. It was in the spring, only, that I noticed the gardens, because of the flowers. One day I saw an old man at his window, leaning on the railing. It was mild out and he was looking. After I understood that he was seeking the gazes of passers-by on his flowers. I looked at the red flowers, and I looked at him, him. He had a victorious smile, triumphant. I smiled too, somewhat as I had learned, but I smiled a bit too long, and he froze suddenly, the old man. He was ashamed, I think, and afraid too, perhaps.

I don't know when the crowd will leave the square. I'm lost. All alone. I need someone beside me, not speaking.

Often, thus, we remained without speaking, she and I, the girl, and me. I liked her solidity especially; even in silence. I felt her like that. We must have appeared solid both of us.

The knees passed by. So much difference among the legs. I'm so low, so near to the earth, so squat, now, that they could almost trample me. I am on the step luckily, at the edge of the street; but if their ranks suddenly swell, overflow, they will really manage to trample me. I'll be lost like this in the midst of the crowd, recaptured by them. Walking is a protection, an edifice. Fragile. Shards of mica on the stone shine in the sun. It's an almost unbearable shimmer. I know there exists a certain continuity between this stone and the entire face of the girl. Perhaps the roundedness erosion has given to the stone at the same time as a hardness, a violent glare.

I was no longer expecting an end to our story. We could have lived longer. Pass on now to another woman, further along, later. It will come slowly. Unless I remain here, on this step waiting for the crowd.

The odors rise in the heat, weigh down, harden in the fabric of my shirt. Hope for sleep.

Say everything again, and finally stop telling. Remember

everything that happened, but not like that. Everything becomes blurred, so inexact. No more affair, no more narrative. Several images that pass by, gestures that return in my sweat, obliteration. Everything is viscous. I'm no longer thinking of the little woman. I'm not really thinking of her anymore. Already she is lost.

He paints monsters. I had never noticed that there were monsters, everywhere. Now I know. They are very real monsters. A woman walks along a wall in the wind, a gray wall, without end. At the very top of the wall, there are from time to time long narrow meshed windows, The woman's face is disproportionately enlarged beginning at the nose. Her ears hang. A crowd walks behind her. Not an intact face. No balance. Each face has a particular deformation. The elements of the face are enlarged, or diminished to the point of disappearing, or else are only indicated by enormous gaping holes, in decomposed flesh.

He paints monsters. It's not true, I've expressed myself poorly. He is too sensitive. He's a beautiful painter. He knows and he likes what is beautiful. That's all his fingers can create. How is it that I see these monsters, that he throws them at my face, that he plunges my hands into that hideous flesh. He doesn't understand what I say to him. He never goes out. He doesn't see the people along the walls. He doesn't take sides, it seems. He rejects real monsters, those that exist. I'm the one, in the colors, who reveals them, who hollows them out. They all come out of him. Where exactly. He is unaware of that too of course. He simply manifests. Out of calm, only violence springs. It's powerful. It can burst apart immobilities, rhythms. I say that it can, as though it were but a possibility. Yet I'm sure of its action. They all feel implicated. They burst from inside. They don't forgive him the revelation, the contact. One day they will kill him. They're preparing a violent death for him. A refinement of suffering. An odious assassination. In fact there are many such assassinations, these days.

I'm not the only one who knows. He too knows it. I cannot say whether he is preparing himself, but he is always on the defensive. For example, for a long time he has refused to speak. He is silent. There is no point speaking of eloquence and it has no real importance. They could prevent him from being quiet, but they don't dare. They too are afraid because there have been precedents and the results are known.

So, for now, they accept. But not for long, probably. Soon they will act.

They were both sitting at the table, on each side. They avoided looking at one another. They continued to speak to one another, thus, at a distance. One might have believed they couldn't hear one another. And yet the dialogue they were establishing was precise, incisive—a whole series of questions, volleyed back and forth like bullets, light questions, precious.

For most people, around them, it made no sense, and yet several tables away, the other one didn't miss any of their talk. He acquiesced sometimes with his head, leaned forward as well, ready to respond, when one of the two manifested the slightest hesitation.

It concerned a disease, that was afflicting one of them—but which one.

It concerned a search, undertaken by one of them—perhaps the same.

With regard to this, one can provide several details. He'd gone, the night before, to knock on doors, gently at first, harder and harder, very rapidly. The people had pounced on him. He'd been placed in a room, after having been hit—a room with gray walls, perfidious. They left him there for a long time. He'd started to think of other things—his mother, walking on the wall—the boat leaving the harbor, by the canal, behind the minuscule little red and black tug—the page of the book he'd been reading the night before, the page he'd seized, suddenly, because it seemed to jump out at his face, tearing his eyes out, flaying him alive. He'd torn it up, then thrown it in the water, and it had floated too long. Longer than it ought to have done. He didn't know exactly why he had wanted it to sink more quickly; sometimes things like that happen, sudden desires, but which we can do nothing about, because they are stories that are not within our power. For example, he thought of the days of heat, of exhaustion, when after a long day, he was on his way home, then, toward the boulevard, when there were only several hundred meters left, he wished he could be lifted from the earth, and transported all the way to the door, and this desire was so strong, that he closed his eyes, stopped, wavered on his legs, and walked in an automatic dream, all the way to the house; on his arrival, he was almost numb, vanquished. The magic never worked until the end.

What had he done in that room. It wasn't clear, actually.

He was perhaps the one who was sick, and spoke thus of his illness. But nothing is less certain.

The other one, further on, had an opinion about this, most likely.

Despite everything, in this manner of asking questions, one ended up no longer knowing who this—incredible— story had happened to because in fact, no one took their conversation seriously. The faces had, for the most part, skeptical expressions. They exchanged looks of understanding, smiles full of irony.

Both of them, or rather, all three, attached no importance to it. They were elsewhere, probably, but together, nonetheless, so bound among one another, so well caught in the same net, the same trap.

I saw him fall into the water earlier. The wind rose, suddenly. The sea passed over the first dock, lower down. He was higher, above. The sea never rises that high. But the wind, with a sudden squall, could carry him off. I was quite aware of it, but it was impossible to go get him. I leaned against, rather was glued, to the wall, the palms of my hands flattened as much as possible against it.

Days and nights, I passed by there. I was immediately interested in him. But I didn't think I could be so attached. I had in a sense taken possession of him, a distant possession of course, somewhat occult, I mean, in relation to the others—a relation of him to me.

We changed together, he became bigger, and me, little by little, I lost my voice. It became weaker and weaker. We each noticed the change separately, I suppose.

On my way past, I was calling him, by tender and stupid names, to myself.

I also told him all the important events of my life.

I gave him extraordinary powers.

I was saddened not to see him if only for an instant each day.

I was afraid of losing him.

I lived with his memory. I said We.

I questioned him. I said "you see, there, the pink house, it's ugly, or else it's simple, what do you think of it," "what does a piece of wood that has travelled extensively feel, a ship's mast for example."

Always sweet stupidities. It wasn't serious. Think of all the events; look at the others a bit, too.

I am being torn from you. You are being carried away. Whoever it is, the wind, the sea, it's worse than anything.

You're going to drown. And I'm watching, without doing anything, without saying anything, on principle, because I must observe the rule. And what if I didn't want to anymore. I can still throw myself with you, grab hold of you. If it were possible.

The old men speak among themselves, with something of a deaf air, somewhat sleepy. They lift their heads back. They acquiesce. They illuminate several things more. We too, we have finished illuminating. It's too late. My nails screech against the wall; the wall on the other side of the dock. We knew it was so beautiful, both of us, ochre, an almost red ochre. I don't see it anymore, since my back is glued to it, and my nails dully skid there.

You think I look like an enormous insect, thus, quartered against this wall. You are perhaps thinking of something else—what. You call me. I hear. But to reply, I have no more voice, not for me, not for you. Nailed, here, I must remain, because I am good for nothing now, nothing. So I suffer because you are being carried off.

You didn't say whether anyone could do anything for you. That, I could have done, helped you through an intermediary. That is perhaps what you wanted, out of discretion. But I didn't know it in time.

Stop. It's important—important—you mustn't miss this, the last moments. But you don't like that. You want to go quickly. You let yourself be carried, removed, killed. And me, in the world that veers behind you, only later will I have the strength to hold you back, only later, after the others—forgive me—when they will have taught me how to stop a piece of earth torn off by the wind—a finished man, a failure, a shadow, a song, a last song—a whole dumbfounded world, which exits from the second dock, into the sea.

Can one admit to having come to an end, when one doesn't know, when one hasn't learned, ever, to write that word, End; to put it at the center, in the middle, to protect it, not leave it alone somewhere, isolated. I say end, I say that it's over, quite finished, this time. I'll not say another thing, I won't repeat anymore, ceaselessly. I'm in the completely dark room, completely dark with this thick night of wishes; because I always wish for that thickness, but rarely does the world, do things, bother to go all the way to the end. There is often a lack of strength, of extremism. One puts one's hand there, one's arm; one would like to put one's body, the whole body, dive in, but there's no way to do it, as it were, ever. It is said that it's luck, people hold forth about it. Me, I'm just in this big black room. How can I know it's big; there's no point starting with the questions. I spoke of them. They're around me. They're restless, half-dead, at least very ironic, already, and the things, so close to me, which surround me, enclose me in a prison. I take one, I throw it in the night. It returns, destroys the equilibrium of the others, which fall in an enormous din around me, smothering my little noise, the sizzling, in my ears, my hands. I'm used to being here. This is the way I began, in this space, bigger and bigger. Arms outstretched, to begin with, one touches the walls—tranquility—and then grazes, less and less. Everything becomes bigger. There is no end to covering the space. And the time required to return to the same point, at the center, it causes so much fear, that it is best not to begin to move, to be content with inventing the rest, peacefully. But since in the distance cries can be heard, one rises, then goes; modestly, it's true; and even sometimes an effort is required. One gropes along. As on the road to hell, there are circles, with different sensations. A whole mythology is registered which could serve as nourishment, at least, one imagines it thus.

I like order. I've put everything in its place, as I believed— in my head—as I thought it should be. Then everything became immobile—idiotically. I would have liked on the contrary for them to continue to move, to move, to live. But it didn't go together. I was then obligated to stop neatening; also in this chaos, I don't know where I am anymore, the only point, the sole marker, is this penetrating night, in this room, where I am, without anyone else, which is quite important. I'm alone here—everyone will think it's bad; it causes dreams—it's true. The dreams arrive, very quickly, with the slightest quiver. To understand, they repeat ceaselessly, you must go out, see the world. I did what they said of course. But I don't know how, treacherously, it always comes back, this moment when despite everything, I find myself here, in the dark. Once more a cycle, another one; back at the same point. No one will come; no one can come, it's nothing to fear, if that is what I fear. Such silence, sometimes. And, strangely, recognizing oneself, in the silence; one's own echo, as in a mirror. A reversal of the situation; no need anymore for them to be here, for them to come near, very near, to see my face, to see the end. That's enough, I am enough for myself, because of the silence, there, all alone, in the dark. I exploded in the world, amid them, without discretion. Now I'm finding calm again, or rather, nothing that can resemble it, in sum, since it's necessary still, still for a long time, to testify that there is no end to this torment. It's what pulls me along, sweeps me away. The whirling—sometimes shimmering images, sometimes hollow ideas, but heavy; terrors also; but not without hope, because still I go on. It's already a lot to go on, most don't realize it. I could let go, slacken my hands, let them slide along the ropes, or choose something else, softer, easier; and even sometimes, listen to their reassuring words. They also think it necessary for me to deny many things I've done. I refuse. I'm attached to my insignificant work of approach. I even clutch at it; every day I trace a word, a dotted line, a sign, to get there. That's the true fear, the only fright, to get gradually nearer, without certainty, to see oneself on that path, the slow pace, imprecise, sometimes distant, to give oneself over to it completely, without restriction, risking oneself completely, without leaving anything behind—to return, retreat—not a piece of earth, a stable space, small though it may be—where one could return to forget. From time to time the world escapes me, flees like water running through my fingers. I hear it near, very near. It surrounds me with its powerful, gigantic presence. But its voice becomes felted. I hear it as though through a screen, a thick glass wall—my eyes, my hands closed. Then, only to my ears, does the voice that is mine alone remain—its hammering, that I would like to make cease, for always. But, ineradicably, it strikes my temples, "march, go on, go on still, march, go on." It's never quiet, and all I hear is it, when, around me, there is silence, in this dark. The voice moans, and I can't stand the moans. I am strong. I want. I don't want to hear the laments, the cries. I press my hands against my ears so as not to hear. But it punctures the space, everywhere, it comes from everywhere, an invasion, running with my blood. I would like with a knife to be able to silence the ferment, liberate some of this flow. But the wounds remain empty. And little by little, I listen to the song, and I have no right anymore, no possibility of forgetting. The bridges burn, the ships catch fire. It is exile, on this road. Others die too, here. There are the remains of their trace around me. I reach them again. The silence is disturbed, formless, a noise, immense, which enters, which burrows, which I must carry as well, accept, a sort of final trial, a last encounter. I salute. My lips tremble, barely articulate, in other languages, other words, whose meanings are yet unknown to me, but I sense, with violence, that they are but suffering and hope and revolt—powerful, powerless, plying—so unbearable. Some, like me, are on a march, and searching, and take that distant road. We cross paths. Together we pass by the river falls, the impacts against the reefs, the slow drops, the unexpected flights. We become attached, toward the approaching arrival; a joint and anguished teaching. Their own language. They know, and suddenly I understand that their voice is the same, and that we are repeating the same words—amazement. I repeat their own words. This voice, mine, it seems now that it is theirs—it isn't clear, but it seems to me—theirs, the same, mine. How to distinguish, exactly, such a slight inequality.

Little by little abandon sets in. One does not die alone, one is killed, by routine, by impossibility, following their inspiration. If all this time, I have spoken of murder, sometimes half camouflaged, it's because of that, that way of killing.

As with a burin, in copper, I must engrave the last words, at the center of a drawing that ought to translate calm, serenity, and also all this time lived and swallowed. But I hesitate, too full of worry, before these definitive words, after which, I will be, once and for all, in full existence, and for the last time, without extension, with the vague idea yet of a contamination of the world, of the disease which afflicts us all.

I still question what I have said, what there was to say. Nothing perhaps. The voice sufficed; it's possible. The invention of differences, agreements, tones, is the work of an entire life, when I am just beginning, I scarcely dare begin mine.

Stop myself—but how—find the last word of speech, when everything is linked, this minute and the next, one breath and the other, flow. Flow.

But weariness also arrives; coldly, I become weary. It isn't only the suddenly arisen question, of the last word, the last breath, but knowing why, why this long, inconsistent work, which is barely enclosed in my hands, without being able to shape it really, complete it, which escapes me with the irregular rhythm which parts my lips. Why the step, not just mine, one in front of the other, but the twisted, entangled step, barely a step, so to speak, in any case unrecognizable, to myself as well, the gait, to the smothered coherence, hidden, that every morning I try to bring to light with my hands, my whole hands. Bring to light. I dive, I tear with my nails, there, inside. And to finish, toward that very end. That is the question I have not yet managed to kill; these doubts in morning, which will still be there after, because, in spite of everything, all I did was try. Such a humble attempt, that I must once more beg myself for this daily operation's charity, to continue living. No it isn't finished. There's more to hear, hear the voice, the questions, encourage oneself, protect oneself, struggle as well to go all the way to the end, with that immense cowardice of preferring words, their edifice, to the small, inconceivable, gesture, that I am not yet able to make. Don't slide just yet, keep holding back until the choice, or rather refuse that choice, that possibility. Pains, taking pains. I walk stumbling, and the completely dark room doesn't yet empty itself of the incessant echo of my steps—my uncertain feet, which seek, seek in the sand, slowly, the end.

Born in Rostrenen in 1940, Danielle Collobert left Bretagne for Paris at the age of eighteen where she worked in an art gallery and self-published her first poems in a book entitled *Chants des guerres* (1961). Both of Collobert's parents, and her aunt, who survived deportation to Ravensbrück, were members of the Résistance during World War II. Herself a supporter of Algerian independence, Collobert joined the FLN (the Algerian National Liberation Front), precipitating her exile in Italy, during which time she completed work on *Meurtre*, first published in 1964 by Éditions Gallimard with the unwavering support of Raymond Queneau. She worked for *Révolution africaine*, a short-lived journal created at the end of the Algerian war. Collobert's extensive travels, to Czechoslovakia, Indonesia, Bolivia, Ecuador, Venezuela, Mexico, Spain, Greece, Egypt, etc., did not prevent her from becoming a member of the group formed around Jean-Pierre Faye and the journal, *Change*. Her other works include *Dire I et II* (1972), a radio play the following year, *Polyphonie*, aired by France Culture, *Il donc* (1976) and *Survie* (1978). Upon her return from a trip to New York, Danielle Collobert took her own life in a hotel in Paris on her thirty-eighth birthday. Her complete works, in two volumes, edited by Françoise Morvan, augmented by several unpublished texts, were published by P.O.L. in 2005. Collobert's other works available in English, include *It Then* and *Notebooks, 1956-1978*, published respectively by O Books and Litmus Press, and translated with great sensitivity by Norma Cole.

Nathanaël is the author of a score of books written in English or French, including *Sisyphus, Outdone. Theatres of the Catastrophal*, *Carnet de somme*, *We Press Ourselves Plainly*, and *L'injure*. *Je Nathanaël* exists in self-translation, as does the essay of correspondence, *Absence Where As (Claude Cahun and the Unopened Book)*, first published in French as *L'absence au lieu*. Nathanaël's translations include works by Édouard Glissant, Catherine Mavrikakis and Hilda Hilst, the latter in collaboration with Rachel Gontijo Araújo. Recognized by a PEN Translation Fund fellowship, Nathanaël's translation of Hervé Guibert's *The Mausoleum of Lovers* will be published by Nightboat Books in 2014. She lives in Chicago.

OTHER LITMUS PRESS TITLES

Then Go On, Mary Burger, $15

I Want to Make You Safe, Amy King, $15

O Bon, Brandon Shimoda, $15

How Phenomena Appear to Unfold, Leslie Scalapino, $24

Beauport, Kate Colby, $15

Time of Sky & Castles in the Air, Ayane Kawata, $18
translated by Sawako Nakayasu

Portrait of Colon Dash Parenthesis, Jeffrey Jullich, $15

Hyperglossia, Stacy Szymaszek, $15

From Dame Quickly, Jennifer Scappettone, $15

Face Before Against, Isabelle Garron, $15
translated by Sarah Riggs

Animate, Inanimate Aims, Brenda Iijima $15

Fruitlands, Kate Colby, $12

Counter Daemons, Roberto Harrison, $15

Emptied of All Ships, Stacy Szymaszek, $12

Inner China, Eva Sjödin, $12
translated by Jennifer Hayashida

The Mudra, Kerri Sonnenberg, $12

Another Kind of Tenderness, Xue Di, $15
translated by Keith Waldrop, Forrest Gander, Stephen Thomas,
Theodore Deppe, and Sue Ellen Thompson

Euclid Shudders, Mark Tardi, $12

Notebooks: 1956–1978, Danielle Collobert, $12
translated by Norma Cole

The House Seen from Nowhere, Keith Waldrop, $12

PUBLISHED IN COLLABORATION WITH BELLADONNA BOOKS

NO GENDER: Reflections on the Life & Work of kari edwards
edited by Julian Talamantez Brolaski, erica kaufman, and E. Tracy Grinnell, $18

Bharat jiva, kari edwards, $15

Four From Japan: Contemporary Poetry & Essays by Women
translated and with an introduction by Sawako Nakayasu, $14

www.litmuspress.org